World of Reading

LEVEL 1

STAR WARS

AT-AT ATTACK!

WRITTEN BY CALLIOPE GLASS

ART BY PILOT STUDIO

ABDO
Spotlight

Disney

LUCASFILM
PRESS

Los Angeles • New York

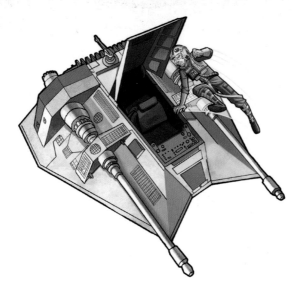

ABDOPUBLISHING.COM

Reinforced library bound edition published in 2018 by Spotlight, a division of ABDO, PO Box 398166, Minneapolis, Minnesota 55439. Spotlight produces high-quality reinforced library bound editions for schools and libraries. Published by Disney • Lucasfilm Press, an imprint of Disney Book Group.

Printed in the United States of America, North Mankato, Minnesota.
042017
092017

THIS BOOK CONTAINS
RECYCLED MATERIALS

PUBLISHER'S CATALOGING-IN-PUBLICATION DATA

Names: Glass, Calliope, author. | Pilot Studio, illustrator.
Title: Star wars: AT-AT attack! / writer: Calliope Glass ; art: Pilot Studio.
Other titles: AT-AT attack!
Description: Reinforced library bound edition. | Minneapolis, Minnesota : Spotlight, 2018. | Series: World of reading level 1
Summary: Luke Skywalker and friends face off against the Empire's dreaded AT-ATs to defend their rebel base on Hoth.
Identifiers: LCCN 2017936171 | ISBN 9781532140532 (lib. bdg.)
Subjects: LCSH: Skywalker, Luke (Fictitious character)--Juvenile fiction. | Star Wars fiction--Comic books, strips, etc.--Juvenile fiction. | Superheroes--Juvenile fiction. | Graphic novels--Juvenile fiction.
Classification: DDC [E]--dc23
LC record available at https://lccn.loc.gov/2017936171

Spotlight
· A Division of ABDO
abdopublishing.com

The planet Hoth
was very, very cold.
Nobody wanted
to live there.

It was the perfect place
for Luke, Han, Leia,
and the rebel army
to hide.

They were hiding
from Darth Vader.

Vader sent robots into
space to find
the secret rebel base.
One of the robots found it.

Vader sent his AT-ATs
to attack the rebels.
The rebel base was
not safe anymore.

Princess Leia
told all the rebels
to fly away.

But she chose to leave last
to make sure the rebels
left safely. Han and C-3PO
stayed with her.

Luke wanted to
protect the base.
The rebels needed
time to escape.

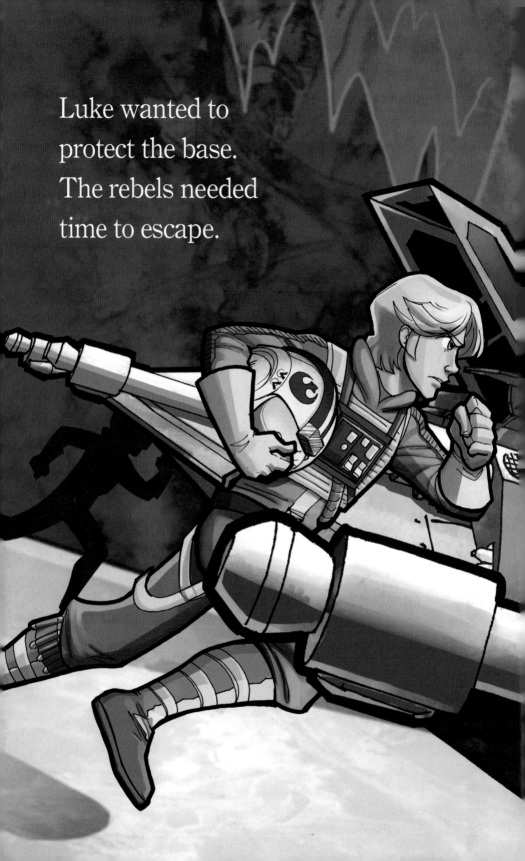

Luke hopped into
a fast ship.

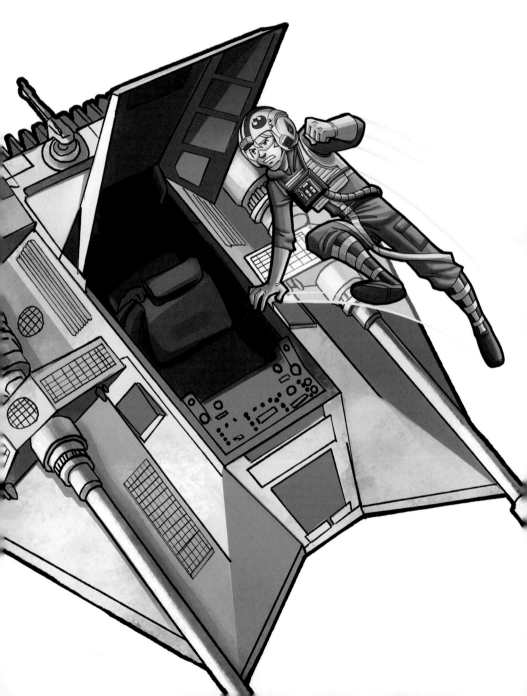

He flew out
to attack the AT-ATs.

The AT-ATs were strong.
Luke tried shooting
at them,
but nothing happened.

While Luke fought the AT-ATs,
Han, Leia, and C-3PO
ran to Han's ship.

But Han's ship was not working.
The motor would not start.

Leia was annoyed.
She thought Han's ship
was a bucket of bolts.

Han and his friend, Chewie,
tried to fix the ship.

They were running
out of time.

Luke needed to
stop the AT-ATs.

Luke and his friends
used cables to trip an AT-AT.

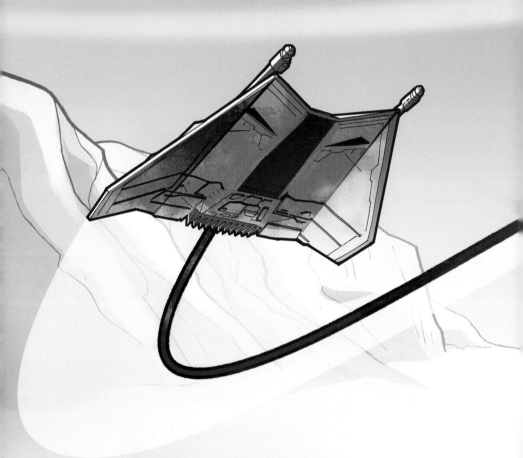

The AT-AT fell down.
Then it exploded!

Luke used
his lightsaber
to stop another AT-AT.

Luke had saved the day!

Darth Vader arrived
at the base.

Vader and his troops
fired at Han's ship.

But at the very last minute . . .

. . . Han's ship
finally started.

Han and Leia flew away.
Luke saw their ship escape.
Luke smiled.
They were all safe!

Their base was destroyed,
but the rebels had
escaped to fight another day.